Billy Burger
MODEL CITIZEN

Billy Burger, Model Citizen is published by
Stone Arch Books,
A Capstone Imprint
1710 Roe Crest Drive
North Mankato, Minnesota 56003
www.mycapstone.com

Library of Congress Cataloging-in-Publication Data
Sazaklis, John, author.
  Jumping for junk food / by John Sazaklis; illustrated by Lee Robinson.
      pages cm. — (Billy Burger, model citizen)
  Summary: His parents have placed the perpetually hungry Billy on a strict diet—no junk
food—and despite the trouble it causes him, it looks like he will be in shape for the annual
school jump-a-thon—which is interrupted by a trio of teenage thieves.
  ISBN 978-1-4965-2586-4 (library binding)
  ISBN 978-1-4965-2683-0 (paperback)
  ISBN 978-1-4965-2687-8 (eBook)
1. Junk food—Juvenile fiction. 2. Low-calorie diet—Juvenile fiction. 3. Rope skipping—Juvenile
fiction. 4. Families—Juvenile fiction. 5. Elementary schools—Juvenile fiction. 6. Conduct of
life—Juvenile fiction. [1. Junk food—Fiction. 2. Diet—Fiction. 3. Rope skipping—Fiction.
4. Family life—Fiction. 5. Schools—Fiction. 6. Conduct of life—Fiction.] I. Robinson, Lee
(Illustrator), illustrator. II. Title.
  PZ7.S27587Ju 2016
  813.6—dc23
  [Fic]   2015028424

Book design by: Ted Williams
Illustrations by: Lee Robinson
Photo credit: Teekay, page 94

Printed in the United States of America in Stevens Point, Wisconsin.
092015   009222WZS16

Billy Burger
MODEL CITIZEN

JUMPING FOR JUNK FOOD

BY JOHN SAZAKLIS

STONE ARCH BOOKS
a capstone imprint

TABLE OF CONTENTS

CHAPTER 1
T.G.I.F. 9

CHAPTER 2
Button Bullet 17

CHAPTER 3
**The Doctor Will
See You Now** 25

CHAPTER 4
**Only the Good
Diet Young** 31

CHAPTER 5
Sticky Fingers 39

CHAPTER 6
Billy Burger: Troublemaker 47

CHAPTER 7
School Rules! 55

CHAPTER 8
Let the Games Begin 63

CHAPTER 9
Fund-Racing 71

CHAPTER 10
Jump Day 77

CHAPTER 11
Billy Burger: Model Citizen 83

HEY, WHAT'S UP?

MY NAME IS
BILLY BURGER.

Nice to meet you! If you're reading this, you have good taste in books. Now that I know something about you, how about I tell you something about me?

I live with my family in a medium-sized house, in a little town called Hicksville, in the big state of New York. Our medium-sized house got much smaller the same time my family got a little bigger—when my baby sister, Ruby, was born. She's kind of cute . . . if you like stinky, smelly, noisemakers!

My parents both work at the Hicksville Police Department. Pretty cool, huh? Dad is a detective. Mom is a criminal psychologist. Together, they solve mysteries and catch troublemakers. Now that I think about it, that isn't much different than taking care of me!

But I wouldn't call myself a troublemaker, exactly. I prefer the term *adventurer*. I'm always looking for interesting things to do or discover because I get bored easily. I think it's because I have an overactive imagination.

(Want to know what's more overactive than my imagination? My appetite! I love to eat, and sometimes I think about that more than anything else. Seriously. I'll try anything . . . twice!)

I usually don't go on adventures alone. My partner in crime is also my best friend, Teddy. He lives a few houses down from me on the same block. I'm always trying to think of fun things for us to do together!

When I get an idea, it is usually awesomely epic. Unfortunately, my ideas don't always go as planned, and that's when I get in trouble.

But I'm working on that.

I'm working on being a better person, a better student, a better everything. Just like my grandpa, William Burger—the Hero of Hicksville. He's sort of a legend in our town. He did good deeds and inspired others to do the same.

And like Grandpa, I'm going to do just that.

I'm going to become **BILLY BURGER: MODEL CITIZEN!**

1
T.G.I.F.

"**FINALLY!** It's Friday! We're free!" I shout. I run down the sidewalk, enjoying the sunny afternoon.

The bus driver just dropped off Teddy and me at our bus stop. Our stop is only a block away from where I live, and Teddy is staying with me until his parents get home.

"Our awesomely epic weekend awaits!" I say.

"I'll race you to your house," Teddy says. "Last one there has to do the other's homework!"

SAY WHAT?!

There is no way I'm doing more homework than I have to.

"You're on!" I shout and run as fast as I can.

Teddy picks up steam and catches up to me.

Then he passes me as quick as a flash.

Suddenly my side aches, so I stop to catch my breath. I'm not even thinking about the extra homework right now, I'm just trying not to throw up.

"OOF," I pant, plopping down on Old Man Withers' front yard.

I fall on my back, but my schoolbag is so bulky that I tip over onto my side.

Teddy circles back around. "Are you okay, man?" he asks.

"Yeah," I wheeze. "Must be . . . my heavy . . . backpack." I try to wriggle out of it, but I'm stuck.

"You remind me of a beached whale." Teddy laughs.

"Hey!" I shout. "Don't make me spray you with my blowhole." I cover one nostril and prepare to shoot a snot rocket at my friend.

Teddy puts his hands up. "Dude! I surrender!" he cries.

"Good. Now . . . help me . . . out of this thing . . . please," I grunt.

Teddy pulls the straps off my arms and chucks the schoolbag onto the grass.

I sit up and start to breathe normally again. "Guess I'm stuck doing a double dose of homework now," I say.

"Nah, man, forget about it," Teddy replies.

I pull down my sleeve and wipe the sweat off my forehead. "What is it, like a thousand degrees out here?" I ask.

Teddy shrugs. "Feels okay to me," he says.

He lies down on the grass and looks up at the sky. After a moment he says, "Fridays really are the best days."

"Totally," I reply.

"We don't have to do anything!" Teddy adds.

"I beg to differ," I say. I rub my hands together like a mad scientist. **"MWA-HA-HA-HA-HA-HA!"**

"What? What?" Teddy asks.

"I have the latest episode of *Super Samurai from Outer Space* saved on our TV," I say.

"Oh, well, we obviously have something to do. We're watching that!" Teddy exclaims. "Duh!"

● ● ●

Teddy and I walk the rest of the way to my house. When we get inside, we dump our schoolbags near the door and take off our shoes.

"Anybody home?" I yell.

"I'm upstairs, honey," my mom calls out. "Changing Ruby's diaper."

"P-U!" I holler back. "Teddy and I are staying down here where the air is fresher!"

I barely get my words out when we hear a loud **GRRRUMBLE!**

"What was that?" Teddy asks.

His eyes are wide with fright.

"You don't have a pit bull, do you?" he asks nervously. "Those things terrify me!"

"Yes, Teddy, I have a pit bull," I say, rolling my eyes. "And it's right behind you!"

"AAAH!" Teddy screams.

"Relax," I say. "It was just my stomach telling me it's snack time."

"Oh, right!" Teddy cries. "I forgot that your stomach has a mind of its own."

"Yeah, so let's get something to eat," I say.

As we head into the kitchen I ask, "So, Teddy, we know Friday is the best day, but what is the best time of day?"

"Snack time!" Teddy says.

"That's right!" I reply. "Other correct answers would have been breakfast, lunch, dinner, and dessert."

Teddy laughs.

If it isn't obvious, I really like to eat. Probably because I'm always hungry!

"So what kind of snacks do you have?" Teddy asks.

"Let's have a look-see, shall we?" I say as I open the pantry door.

Teddy whistles. "Whoa, dude!" he exclaims. "It's like the Cave of Wonders in here."

My friend pushes me aside and starts pulling boxes and bags off the shelves.

"I mean, you got all the good stuff: Cheese puffs, double fudge brownies, chocolate chunk cookies, lime-flavored tortilla chips . . . It just goes on and on! Man, my mom would never let me eat half this stuff!"

"Mine either," I say. "But we lucked out, see? My parents stocked up for this big party they were going to have last week. Then Ruby got sick with an ear infection. The bad part was that she was up all night, screaming and crying and pulling her ears. And Mom and Dad had to cancel the party. But the good part is now we get to have a party of our own!"

"WOO-HOO! PAR-TEE!" Teddy cheers.

We grab as many snacks as we can carry and walk to the den. Teddy and I get comfortable on the couch, while I search for our cartoon show on the DVR.

"Aha!" I announce. "Here it is! The next epic episode!"

Super Samurai from Outer Space is a show about four Samurai brothers from ancient Japan. They have the power to travel through the galaxy at the speed of light. Their mission is to fight mutants and monsters trying to destroy the universe.

I lean back and tear open a bag of barbeque-flavored potato chips. The sweet and salty smell fills the air.

I waft the aroma into my face and inhale the tastiness. "My taste buds are ready to party too!" I exclaim.

2
Button Bullet

CHOMP! CRUNCH! MUNCH! GULP!

Teddy and I stuff our faces with potato chips and
barely even stop to breathe. We inhale them all before
the first commercial break. Nothing but crumbs are left.

Carefully, I tip the bag upside down and shake them
into my mouth.

"What's next?" Teddy asks, wiping potato chip dust
off his T-shirt.

"How about the chocolate chunk cookies?" I suggest.

"Excellent idea. Let's dunk the chunk!" Teddy replies.
"Got milk?"

"Yes, sir," I say.

Right as Teddy and I enter the kitchen, my mom shows up.

"What are you doing?" she asks, surprised. "You're not eating all that junk food are you?"

I quickly hide the box of cookies behind my back and pass it to Teddy. He scoops it up out of my hand and runs into the den with it.

"See?" I say holding up my empty hands. "**NO JUNK FOOD!** I just came into the kitchen for two nice, cold glasses of milk."

My mom looks at me suspiciously.

"Then what's all over your face and hands?" she asks.

Uh-oh, I think. *Must be all that barbecue chip dust.*

Suddenly an ear-piercing wail fills the air.

"WAAAAAAAH!" Ruby is crying in her crib.

Mom sighs and goes back upstairs.

"Phew," I say, wiping my brow. "Saved by the screech!"

I get our glasses of milk and join Teddy in the den. Then we go to town on the double chocolate chunk cookies. The poor things didn't even know what hit them.

Soon after, my stomach starts to feel funny. It feels overstuffed like a Thanksgiving turkey.

Maybe if I lean back a bit, I won't feel so much pressure, I think.

Just as I try to get comfortable, I hear a loud **POP!**

The button on my jeans rips off and flies across the room like a bullet!

"What the—?" Teddy cries.

"Did you see—?" I say.

The button bounces off of my dad's model World War II plane and zips back toward us. It slaps Teddy in the face, leaving an imprint on his forehead.

"OW!" he yells.

Then we both stare at each other thinking, *Did that just happen?*

We laugh and laugh until we are red in the face and tears are streaming down our cheeks.

"Billy, your belly is a deadly weapon!" Teddy gasps.

I'm laughing so hard that I barely notice that the model airplane is still teetering on the brink of the shelf.

"Oh, no, the *Hawker Fury!*" I cry and leap off the couch.

The *Hawker Fury* was a British biplane and Dad's favorite model. If it breaks, I'll be facing his fury for sure!

I rush to catch the plane as it tips over the edge.

"ACK!" I cry and reach out my hands.

But guess what? Since I no longer have a button on my jeans, they drop right to my ankles and I trip over them!

THUD!

I bang my knees and slide across the rug.

WHOOSH!

Luckily, the model airplane lands right in the palm of my hands.

"PHEW!" I say, breathing a sigh of relief.

"HAHAHAHAHAH!" Teddy cackles. "I see London, I see France! I see Billy's underpants!" he sings.

Teddy falls off the couch, laughing even harder.

"Oh, knock it off," I say, pulling up my jeans.

Holding my pants up with one hand, I return Dad's model airplane onto the shelf.

This situation would be funnier if it were happening to Teddy and not me.

Looking down at my pants, I see that the fabric has ripped where my button used to be.

"Oh, man!" I complain. "My pants are ripped! How am I gonna fix them? I don't know how to sew!"

Teddy looks thoughtful. "You could try stapling them," he says.

"How 'bout I staple your big trap shut?" I might get a little rude when I'm embarrassed.

Suddenly my mom calls me from the kitchen.

"Billy, why is the refrigerator handle all sticky and greasy?"

She finds us in the den and looks around the room at the empty snack bags and boxes.

"You ate **ALL** this junk food?" she gasps.

I stare down at my feet.

"Not exactly," I reply. "Teddy helped."

Teddy shoots me a nasty look. "Uh, I think I hear my mom calling me," he says, cupping his ear. "Yup, that's her all right!"

"I don't hear any—" my mom starts.

But Teddy picks up his backpack, slips into his sneakers, and heads for the door. In a flash, he's gone.

Mom folds her arms across her chest. "You know what we said about junk food."

"That it's delicious?" I say.

"No, Billy," she says, rubbing her temples. "That it's unhealthy and too much is bad for you."

How can something that tastes so good be so bad? I say to myself.

And that's when Mom says a bad word that starts with D.

"I think it's time we called the doctor," she says.

"Doctor!" I shout. "Why?"

"So we can talk about your diet," Mom answers. "We need to change a few things around here."

DIET?

SAY WHAT!? That's the other bad D word!

Mom looks down and picks up my button.

"No way around it, young man," she says. "First thing tomorrow morning, we're going to the pediatrician."

3
The Doctor Will See You Now

It's Saturday morning, and I'm lying in bed feeling miserable. Saturday mornings are supposed to be spent sleeping in and then watching Super Samurai cartoons while eating sweet, sugary Super Samurai cereal.

But not this Saturday morning.

Mom made an appointment for me with my pediatrician. (That's a snazzy word for *kid doctor*. Meaning a doctor who works with kids. Not an actual kid that's a doctor.)

Anyway, going to the doctor is no fun at all.

KNOCK-KNOCK. Someone is at my door. I pull the covers over my head and hope that they go away.

No such luck.

"Hey, champ," says my dad. "May I come in?"

"Billy isn't here right now," I yell back. "Leave a message after the beep. **BEEP!**"

The door opens and Dad walks in.

"Smooth," he says, "but I'm not falling for that old trick!"

Dad sits on the edge of my bed.

"I don't have to be a detective to figure out something is wrong. You wanna talk about it?" he says.

My dad is really cool and fun and we get along great. Except for when I get in trouble. Then he's not so fun.

I sit up and look at him.

"Mom's making me go to the doctor, and she's gonna give me a shot with a big needle," I complain. "What if it goes through my arm?"

"Billy, listen to me," Dad says. "The doctor is not going to give you a shot. She is just going to give you a checkup and talk about making some changes in your diet."

"But *whyyyy?*" I whine.

"This is a good thing, actually, little buddy," Dad replies.

"How so?" I ask.

Dad smiles.

"This is a good thing because we all need to change our eating habits—as a family. Ever since Ruby was born, your mom and I didn't have the time and energy to be mindful of our food choices. So you have inspired us to go to the doctor too."

Whoa, my dad is kind of a superhero in real life, so for him to say that I inspired him is a big deal!

"I did that?" I ask.

"Yeah, champ, you did."

Dad puts out his fist, and I bump it. I also start feeling a little better.

"How about I make us a nice, healthy breakfast before you head out?" Dad says.

I finally change out of my pajamas into a pair of sweatpants and my favorite Super Samurai T-shirt for a bit of good luck.

Dad and I enter the kitchen where Mom is feeding Ruby her breakfast. There seems to be more food on Ruby's face than in her mouth.

When she sees me, Ruby smiles. Her two little bottom teeth peek out from her gums. **"EEEEEE!"** she squeals.

PLOP!

A big chunk of oatmeal dribbles out of her mouth and onto her bib.

"I guess Ruby has a food problem too," I say.

• • •

After breakfast my whole family piles into the car. Mom and Dad are in the front while I sit in the back and watch Ruby in her car seat.

Mom drops off Dad at the police station first before taking me to the doctor.

"Have a good day, honey," she says and gives him a kiss . . . **ON THE LIPS**.

"Gross!" I yell and cover my eyes. "I just ate!"

Dad waves good-bye and we drive off.

"Honey, I forgot to tell you," Mom says. "Your regular doctor is away, so we're going to see a new pediatrician today."

"Great," I mumble.

Once we get to the doctor's office, Mom, Ruby, and I hang out in the waiting room. Mom sits on the floor with Ruby, and they play with bright-colored plastic blocks. I sit on a comfy chair with a magazine that has games and puzzles.

Just as I settle in, a nurse appears and says, "Billy Burger? The doctor will see you now."

"Great," I mumble again.

4
Only the Good Diet Young

We follow the nurse down a long hallway, and she brings us to a room at the end. Inside is a frizzy-haired woman with glasses and a white lab coat.

"Hi, Billy, I'm Dr. Nico, your pediatrician," she says. "I like your T-shirt."

To spare you all the boring details, the doctor weighed me on the scale and measured my height. Then she took my blood pressure and listened to my lungs and heart.

Nothing painful or out of the ordinary. I guess that maybe doctors aren't so bad after all.

"Well, Mrs. Burger," Dr. Nico says. "Billy is slightly overweight."

Never mind what I said. Doctors are terrible people!

"He's otherwise healthy," the doctor continues. "But at this age he should be getting at least an hour of physical activity a day."

An hour seems like a long time, especially when running from the bus stop to my house nearly killed me.

"I agree," Mom says. "We're trying really hard to stay active and eat healthy. Unfortunately, these last couple months have been very busy with our new baby, Ruby."

As if on cue, my sister snort-laughs and a big snot bubble pops out of her nose. She tries to lick it with her tongue, but Mom wipes it away with a tissue.

"That is understandable," says Dr. Nico. "I'm providing you with some materials to put on your refrigerator as a reminder. Do you know what this is, Billy?"

She hands me a small poster with a picture of a round plate divided into different sections. In each section are different things to eat. I can't help but notice the vegetables section looks pretty big.

"This is MyPlate," Dr. Nico says. "It's a guide to help you make healthy choices when you eat."

I look at the colorful sections and scratch my head.

"MyPlate is broken down into sections like fruits, vegetables, protein, and grains," she continues.

I look at the poster again and flip it over. The back side is blank.

"Where are the snacks and sweets located?" I ask.

Dr. Nico smiles. "There aren't any."

SAY WHAT?!

I hand the poster back to Dr. Nico.

"This must be *YourPlate*," I say. "Because *MyPlate* would have sweets and treats on it!"

"Billy," my mom says in her behave-yourself voice.

I throw my arms in the air.

"A healthy diet does not consist of many snacks and sweets," Dr. Nico says.

"Oh, come on, Mom!" I cry. "How am I supposed to stop eating. My last name is **BURGER**!"

"William, that's enough!" Mom says.

"Sorry," I say. I probably should have known that getting winded from running from the bus stop to my house was a bad sign. Maybe I didn't want to believe it.

Dr. Nico puts her hand on my shoulder.

"Throughout the galaxy, far and wide, we stand together side by side," she says.

My eyes bug out of my head.

"Hey, that's the Super Samurai secret oath!" I exclaim. "How do you know?"

"I'm a doctor," she replies. "I know a lot of things. Look, Billy, we only want to help you. If we all work together, you'll see results in no time."

I feel a lot better. I'm even a little excited to get started.

You know something? I say to myself. *Doctors are pretty cool.*

● ● ●

After we come home from the doctor's office, Mom tapes the MyPlate poster onto the refrigerator door. Next to it she puts up a paper that has two columns. One says **YES FOODS** and the other says **NO FOODS**.

The **YES FOODS** list has gross things like spinach, brussels sprouts, and fish. And the **NO FOODS** list has delicious things like lollipops, cookies, and cake.

I think something is very wrong with the **NO** list, but Mom and Dad are very strict about following it.

They even start following it themselves.

Dad throws out all the junk food in the house.

"Are you crazy?" I ask.

"Hey, watch that mouth," Dad replies.

"One of the things Dr. Nico said was to set goals," Mom says. "Our first goal is to change some of our food choices."

I exhale and flop onto the sofa.

Ruby thinks this is hilarious and waves her hands in the air. **"EEEEEEE!"** she drools.

What am I gonna do? I think.

I love sitting in class and thinking about hamburgers and waffle fries.

I even have visions of chicken nuggets dancing in my head.

I used to love counting the minutes until lunchtime, but now I'm gonna dread it.

This is going to be torture!

5
Sticky Fingers

So, here I am, one healthy-food week later. I'm sitting at the lunch table with Teddy and our friends Michael and Jason, and the jokes continue.

"Hey, Billy," asks Michael, "what kind of rabbit food did you bring today?"

"Ha-ha, very funny," I say, opening my lunchbox.

I take out my low-sodium turkey and cheese sandwich on whole grain bread and place it next to a little plastic bag full of grapes.

Then I take out another plastic bag with pieces of a long, green vegetable cut up.

"It's not rabbit food," I say. "This is celery, you should try it sometime."

"Oh, I know what celery is," Michael replies. "Because my sister feeds it to her pet rabbit!"

Michael and Jason laugh like it's the funniest thing they've ever heard. I crunch into my celery sticks and shoot them a dirty look.

To be honest, I kinda like eating vegetables. I'm just not going to tell my friends that. I have a reputation to protect!

"Hey, Michael," I say. "How about I trade you my grapes for your pudding cup?"

"No way, dude," he says, guarding the pudding cup with his life. "Stay away!"

"Yeah, keep your gross rabbit food to yourself," Jason adds.

"What are you talking about, man?" I tell Jason. "You've got a bag of raisins right there!"

"Yeah, so?" Jason says.

"Raisins **USED TO BE GRAPES**!" I reply, raising my voice.

Jason picks up his raisins. "So these things used to be grapes?" he asks, scrunching his face.

"Yeah," I say. "And now they're wrinkled and gross. If what I'm eating looks like rabbit food, then what you're eating looks like rabbit poop!"

"EWW!" Jason shouts. He drops his raisins.

Michael laughs and snorts so hard that milk comes shooting out of his nose. **SPLAT!**

"Score!" I shout to Michael, and we high-five.

As my friend wipes up the soggy mess with his napkin, Teddy taps the table with his hands.

"All right, you guys," he says. "Enough with the jokes. We have more important things to discuss."

"Like what?" asks Jason.

"Like yesterday's episode of *Super Samurai from Outer Space*!" replies Teddy.

"Oh, right!" Jason says. "Where they travel to the Meketrex Quadrant and face off against that fire-breathing Sloar!"

"Dude, that Sloar was the coolest monster I have ever seen!" Michael adds, wiping his nose. "With its huge horns and scaly skin and sharp claws—look! I drew a picture of it during class this morning."

"Cool!" I say. "Let me see!"

Michael pulls out a tiny sketchpad from his pocket and shows us the picture.

"Sick!" Jason replies.

Michael is a talented artist. He's going to be famous someday for drawing cartoons or comic books. Or both.

Jason's a really good athlete, and Teddy is a super good actor.

The four of us combined are a terrific team like the Super Samurai. I just gotta figure out what I'm good at . . . aside from getting into trouble and eating junk food.

Mmm.

Junk food.

My mind wanders, and I start thinking about all the wonderful flavors of potato chips. Sour cream and onion, barbeque, cheddar, even salt and vinegar. My taste buds start to tingle. I can feel the saliva forming in the corners of my mouth.

"Yo, Billy!" Teddy shouts.

"Huh?" I say, looking at my friend.

"Yeah, you zoned out and had this glazed look in your eyes," Michael says.

"*Mmm*, glazed . . . like donuts," I reply.

My taste buds start to tingle again.

It's been almost seven days since I had a potato chip. I've almost forgotten what they look like.

I pick up my empty plastic bags and walk over to the recycling bin near the cashier. As if in a trance, I glance over at the bright, colorful snack bags all lined up in a row. The shiny plastic is mesmerizing.

I feel this urge inside my body. It's like a tiny little voice saying, *Go ahead, Billy. What's one bag gonna do to ya? You've been good for six days. Go ahead . . . take it.*

I lick my lips and can feel beads of sweat forming on my forehead. Turning away, I take a deep breath and throw out my garbage.

Then that voice pops into my head again. *Look at all those delicious potato chips. You can't eat just one!*

As if my body is being controlled by someone else, I grab one of the bags and rush back to my lunch table. The guys stare in shock as I tear into the bag like a savage beast and shove a handful of chips into my mouth without thinking.

"**MMMMMM**," I say as I chomp away on the salty, crunchy snack.

I lick my fingers and shovel a second handful into my mouth. The chips are so delicious that I don't notice the two figures walking up behind me.

All of a sudden, a hand grabs my shoulder.

"**GOTCHA!**" yells a voice.

I drop the bag and turn to see the lunch monitor. Standing next to her is the cashier.

"That's him," she says, pointing her finger at me. "That's the thief!"

Suddenly my brain starts working again. My blood turns cold as I realize what happened.

I STOLE THE BAG OF CHIPS!

"On your feet," commands the lunch monitor. "You're going to the principal's office!"

I can feel all eyes on me. Kids are whispering to each other. I can only imagine what they are saying.

There goes Billy Burger—the troublemaker!

The loudmouth!

The thief!

I can feel my cheeks turning red, and I turn around and plead my case.

"It was an accident, I swear! I wasn't thinking clearly. My brain stopped and my body was on auto-pilot!" I tell the lunch monitor. "I will pay for the potato chips, I promise. There is no need to involve Principal Crank."

"No need to involve me in what?" booms a loud voice.

It's Principal Crank.

I should have known better than to say his name out loud. He can probably appear out of nowhere, like an evil spirit conjured up in a horror movie.

Principal Crank is standing behind me. He seems as tall as a tree and wearing a gray suit that matches his gray shoes and gray hair.

The lunch monitor tells him what happened.

Principal Crank rubs his chin and narrows his eyes.

"I see," he says. "Well, William, you certainly know your way to my office. Let's go."

Oh man, this is not my day.

6
Billy Burger: Troublemaker

I follow the principal down the hall. I'm wondering if my new diet has made me space out. I'm just not thinking straight.

I would never steal! Dad told me that stealing is bad. He locks up crooks who steal all the time.

Just for the record, this isn't the first time I've gone to Principal Crank's office. I've been there so many times I'm kind of surprised I don't have my own chair in there. One with my name carved on it.

My grandmother says the reason I get in trouble so much is because I'm very rambunctious. That's a snazzy way to say I'm a wild child. But I am working on calming down a bit.

This little accident is just a small step in the wrong direction.

Once we are inside his office, Principal Crank shuts the door behind us. He sits at his desk, takes a deep breath, and lets out a long sigh.

He does that every time I'm in here.

"Well, William, I must say that this behavior is extremely out of character, even for you," he says very calmly. "Unlike your usual antics, stealing is a very serious offense. Please explain yourself."

"It was an accident," I reply. "I wasn't thinking clearly! Really! I've been eating a lot of fruits and vegetables lately. I think they made me buggy in the head. I didn't mean to steal. I'll pay for them right now."

I dig into my pockets and empty the contents onto Crank's desk; a rubber band, a paper clip, some lint, and a beat-up baseball card. No money.

Principal Crank is starting to lose his cool. "Don't joke around, Mr. Burger. I do not care for jokes!" he says.

Now this is more like the Principal Crank we all know and fear.

"I'm sure your father, the police officer, will not be pleased when he hears about this."

• • •

Well . . . Principal Crank was right. My father was not pleased to hear about this since he had to leave the police station and pick me up from school.

Dad looks very serious and angry when he arrives. He pays for the bag of chips and walks me to the car.

After driving for a while, Dad breaks his silence.

"Stealing?!" he says loudly. "Of all the things, Billy! Stealing? We taught you better than that."

"It was an accident," I say once again. "I was gonna pay for it. I just got distracted because my taste buds were dancing and singing from the deliciousness."

"Billy," my father continues. "Do you know what I was doing today?"

I shrug my shoulders.

"I was interviewing three different shop owners down on Broadway near the town square. Do you know why?"

I shrug again.

"Because each of their stores had been robbed," Dad says, looking at me. "And then I get a call from your principal telling me that my own son is doing the same thing. I just can't believe it."

Dad pulls into our driveway to drop me off.

"Grandma will be watching you and Ruby until Mom and I get home. You and I are going to have a long talk later, you understand?"

"Yes, sir," I mumble.

Dad pats me on the back, and I get out of the car.

Once inside the house, I take off my schoolbag and kick it across the floor.

"Good afternoon, William," says a voice from the living room.

"Good afternoon, Grandma," I reply. "How do you do?"

I greet my grandmother formally when I see her because she says that's proper "etiquette." Which is a snazzy way of saying "nice manners."

Grandma walks over to me and gives me a kiss on the cheek.

"I heard about your . . . situation at school," she says.

"I don't wanna talk about it," I grumble.

"That's fine," she replies. "But I'm going to talk about it anyway. William, your grandfather was a magnificent man. He was a loving husband and father and a decorated war hero. Did you know he was also a model citizen?"

I nod my head yes.

Grandpa was the first William Burger, but he passed away close to when Ruby was born about a year ago. I'm named after him, in case you hadn't guessed it yet. Usually, when I get in trouble, Grandma reminds me of all the good things he did. I get in trouble a lot, so Grandma ends up repeating herself a few times.

"Your grandfather helped the community in many ways. That is why that monument in the Hicksville town square is dedicated to him," Grandma adds.

Right across the library and near the train station is a cool large fountain. It's the William Burger Reflecting Pool. Says so right on a marble plaque at the base. It really is a neat fountain, and I visit it with my family all the time.

"My sweet child, your grandfather was a great man, yes, but he was once a boy just like you. And also just like you, he had a rambunctious spirit and thirst for adventure."

I nod. That sounds like me.

"We all have days when we are not thinking clearly, Billy, even your grandpa. One day, your grandfather was so busy rushing a wounded dog to the vet that he forgot to eat lunch. He picked up a sandwich from a street vendor and left without paying. After he realized his mistake, Grandpa went back the next day and paid for two sandwiches."

"I know stealing is bad. I didn't mean to do it," I repeat.

"My darling child, it's okay to make mistakes as long as you learn from them, and if possible, fix them." Her eyes twinkle as she smiles at me. I start to feel a little better.

"Not only do you carry your grandfather's name, but everything it stands for. And I know that you will honor it as best as you can."

Maybe it's not too late to fix this mess after all.

"You're right, Grandma," I say. "I'm sorry about getting in trouble, and I know that I can prove myself to you, to Mom and Dad, to my school . . . to everybody. I will become Billy Burger, Model Citizen!"

⑦ School Rules!

The next morning I meet Teddy at the bus stop. His eyes are wide with shock.

"Yo, man, I'm surprised you're still alive!" he says. "What happened after you got sent home?"

I fill him in on the details, including the talk I had with Grandma.

"When Dad and Mom came home last night, I expected the worst. I thought they were going to yell at me," I tell him, "but instead Mom suggested that we go for a walk."

"Really?" Teddy asks. "Was it a trick to get you outside so they could lock the door behind you? My brother did that once to me."

"Dude, you fell for that?" I ask. "It's the oldest trick in the book!"

"Whatever," Teddy says. "Enough about me. What happened next?"

"Well, part of my doctor's new goal list is to be more active. So my mom thought this was a good way for us to move as a family." I say that last part and make quotation marks with my fingers because that was how Mom said it.

Another reason to go for a walk was to escort Grandma home, since she lives only a few blocks away. She said she felt like the Queen of Sheba with her own entourage.

"*Hmm,*" says Teddy. "I was expecting you to be grounded for a month."

"Oh, I am," I reply, "No TV, no tablet, no GameBox, nothing. To be honest, it's not as bad as being on this diet. Today's snack is carrot sticks with peanut butter."

"That actually sounds pretty good," Teddy says.

"Yeah, it is," I admit. "I'm definitely over eating junk food for a while especially after yesterday's cafeteria caper."

"So your dad didn't bring you to the police station and lock you up?"

"Ha-ha, very funny," I say. "The truth is, my dad got upset because he says my actions are a reflection on him as a father and a policeman."

Teddy nodded his head. "Well, yeah," he says. "Your dad's a cop and you're a robber."

"I'm **NOT** a robber!" I shout.

But I calm right down.

"Hey, speaking of robbers, that reminds me of what my dad said. Did you know that a couple of shops in the town square had been burglarized?"

"No way!" Teddy says.

"It's kinda scary," I say. "These store owners come into work and find their places trashed and their money and stuff stolen. Dad says they haven't caught any suspects, but one of the shops had a security camera. So they are reviewing the tape for clues."

"Wow, that's kind of awesome, though, you know, aside from the burglaries and stuff."

"Yeah, man. Totally. My dad wouldn't tell me anything else, though."

"I do love a good mystery," Teddy says right as the bus pulls up.

"Ha, yeah," I reply. "Me too."

* * *

When the bus finally arrives, Teddy and I climb aboard. As soon as the other kids see me they start whispering to each other.

I grip my schoolbag and rush all the way to the backseat. Teddy and I sit here so we can look out the back door at the moving traffic. Usually, we make silly faces at the drivers in the cars behind us, but not today.

I'm trying to be on my best behavior and ask myself, *What would Grandpa do?* He probably wouldn't make silly faces, that's for sure.

After a good amount of time, the bus finally pulls up to Fork Lane Elementary School.

Yep, my school is on a street called Fork Lane. It always makes me think of eating. How could it not?

Anyway, once we get inside, Teddy and I walk to our classroom. Our teacher, Mr. Karas, is writing something on the board.

Mr. Karas is a tall man, with a beard and glasses. Sometimes he brings his guitar into class to help us learn by singing songs.

As soon as we are seated, Mr. Karas claps his hands to get us to quiet down.

"May I have your attention, please?" he says. "I have some very exciting news. News so exciting, that it will literally have you jumping for joy!"

Mr. Karas starts jumping up and down. "Come on, everybody," Mr. Karas says. "Jump!"

Teddy is the first one out of his seat. He starts jumping up and down too. I start laughing and join my teacher and my best friend.

"Excellent, Billy and Teddy!" Mr. Karas says. "Who's next?"

Michael and Jason and some of the other kids join in the fun.

Polly, the class know-it-all, raises her hand. "Mr. Karas, did you have jumping beans for breakfast? What are you doing?" she asks.

"I'm jumping for joy, Polly," Mr. Karas answers. Then he starts hopping on one foot. "Now I'm hopping on one foot," he says.

Those of us jumping copy the teacher and hop on one foot. We start laughing even harder.

"Now, class, if you stop to feel your heart, you'll notice it is pumping blood throughout your body," Mr. Karas says. "That's just a small taste of the big news: Fork Lane School is hosting this year's Jump-a-thon. As you all know, the Jump-a-thon is a jump rope competition and fund-raising event sponsored by Hicksville's very own radio station, KHIX. Joining KHIX as entertainment are celebrity fitness guru Robert Summers and his rockin' band, the Jumping Jacks!"

We all stop hopping and start cheering.

"But wait, there's more," Mr. Karas continues. "First prize is a free trip to the Adventuretown amusement park!"

And the class goes wild.

"We've never done anything this cool before," I say to Teddy. "This school rules!"

"True that," he says. "Guess there's a first time for everything."

"Yeah," I reply. "And first prize is going to be **MINE**."

8
Let the Games Begin

"Mom! Dad! Guess what?!" I yell, running into the door after school.

It is a rare occasion when both my parents are home at the same time. Even Ruby is awake and ready for a stroll.

"We're going to head down to the park," Mom says. "Why don't you tell us along the way."

The weather is getting nicer, and part of our new moving-as-a-family routine is to play at the park too.

"What's up, champ?" Dad asks.

"There's gonna be a Jump-a-thon at school," I reply.

"What's that?" Mom asks.

"Mr. Karas describes it as a charity fund-raiser, but basically we jump rope to music all day. Whoever raises the most money wins a trip for their whole family to Adventuretown!"

"That's an excellent idea," Mom says. "Sounds like fun too. How do you raise money?"

"We gotta find people to sponsor us. And since it's a competition, I need to find as many people as possible," I tell my parents. "So far there's you two and Grandma, Aunt Claire and Uncle Cliff, Old Man Withers from next door, Mrs. Beakley from across the street . . . and that's all the people I know with their own money!"

I stop to catch by breath and continue.

"We have a couple weeks to prepare, and I've been dying to go to Adventuretown. I know it costs a lot, but this would be our chance to go!"

"I'm sure we can help out," Mom says.

"Since I started eating differently, my body feels a lot better," I add. "I'm gonna start teaching people how important it is to take care of themselves. Mr. Karas gave us these pamphlets from the charity to pass out to our sponsors. All they do is fill out a form with their donation, and they'll get a certificate for participating."

"Wow, this does sound like a big deal," Dad says.

"Well, yeah," I reply. "The radio station is hosting it. They are bringing in some TV exercise guy named Robert Summers."

"Oh my, Robert Summers!?" Mom yells. "Grandma and I watch him all time. We exercise to his videos!"

Dad smiles at Mom and turns to me. "How about tomorrow I take you into town, and we visit each shop. You can plead your case to the owners and see how generous they can be. Then we'll each buy a jump rope and practice."

"Awesome," I say. "Race you to the end of the block!"

"You're on!" Dad says.

He sprints first, but I catch up to him in no time. I push a little harder, and before I know it, I'm actually passing Dad.

I get to the end of the block first. And this time I make it without collapsing!

My heart is beating fast. I'm gulping mouthfuls of air, but it feels great. I'm feeling good, like nothing can stop me now!

"WOO-HOO!" I cry. "I did it. I won!"

"I'm proud of you, son," Dad says. "If we keep this up, you'll be in tip-top shape for that fund-raiser before you know it."

"That's right," I reply. "Bring on the Jump-a-thon!"

● ● ●

That weekend, Dad drives us to the Hicksville town square so I can start my fund-raising.

"This is gonna be awesome. I'm super pumped!" I say, jumping in my seat.

I brought along the sponsor sheet and pamphlets in my schoolbag. The pamphlets have different tips and information on how to live a healthy life. I already know most of the information, thanks to Dr. Nico.

I look out the window as Dad carefully pulls into the parking lot.

"So where do you want to start first?" he asks.

"Oh, we're starting at the very beginning and hitting every shop till we drop!" I exclaim.

Dad laughs as we exit the car.

The first store at the end of the shopping center is the House of Sweets. It is a coffee shop and bakery.

I can actually smell the sweet aroma of donuts and pastries from across the street.

"*Mmm*, that smells good," I tell Dad. "Wish we could get something to eat!"

"I hear you, Billy," he replies.

As we enter the shop, the little bell over the door jingles. **DING-A-LING!**

The amazing smell is even stronger now.

"**WELCOME**, my friends!" booms a voice.

A stout, round man appears wearing a white apron smeared with chocolate icing. He has curly black hair and a mustache.

"Good morning, Mr. Katsikis," says my father.

"Detective Burger! Long time, no see!" shouts the storeowner. "How come you don't pass by in the morning anymore? Look! Half of you is missing!" Mr. Katsikis playfully pats my dad's tummy.

"Sorry about that, Mr. Katsikis," Dad says. "We've been cutting back on the sweets as a family."

Mr. Katsikis looks at me and smiles even more.

"Oh, hey!" he says. "Is this your partner? Is he a junior detective?!"

"I'm Billy," I say. "Pleased to meet you."

"Now I know I'm in good hands if you're on the case," Mr. Katsikis says, winking.

He guides us to the far side of the store where one of the windows has been boarded up. "Those hooligans smashed my window and broke open the register. I don't keep much in it overnight, but they made a big mess."

"I remember that night a few weeks back," Dad replies. "I got a call on my car radio that the alarm went off in the store. By the time my squad got here, the crooks were gone."

"They took all the cheese danishes and apple turnovers and even the tray of my mama's baklava!" wails Mr. Katsikis.

I glance past him at the display window and think of all the wonderful treats inside. My mouth starts to water.

Willpower, Billy! I think to myself. *Use your willpower and forget the sweets!*

"I'm sorry about your store," I say.

"That's okay, my boy," Mr. Katsikis replies. "The security tape captured the three hooded figures on video. But all we could see was that they wore black hoodies with a symbol on the back."

"When we looked at the footage," Dad says, "we discovered that the symbol was a flaming comet. That's the emblem of the high school sports teams, the Hicksville Comets."

"So the thieves are teenagers?" Mr. Katsikis asks.

"I cannot confirm nor deny that until we have more information," Dad answers. "But it's all in a day's work."

"Then let's get to work," the baker says. "How may I help you?"

"Well, actually, Billy wanted to conduct some business with you," my dad says.

I feel a little embarrassed asking for money from a man who just got robbed, but I explain the Jump-a-thon to Mr. Katsikis. "Would you like to be one of my sponsors?" I ask.

"Of course!" he says, patting me on the back. "What you are doing is for a good cause. More young people should behave like you. You are a good boy! Let me get my checkbook!"

Mr. Katsikis disappears into the kitchen.

I look at my dad and smile. "It sure feels good to do good," I say.

9 FUND-RACING

Dad and I leave the House of Sweets and head to our next destination: The Little Shop of Flowers. It is a tiny, little flowershop owned by a really nice florist named Mr. Roeser.

I'm still feeling the rush of excitement from getting my first sponsor.

Dad got two iced teas and two fat free muffins for us to eat. Fund-raising sure builds up an appetite.

When we enter the Little Shop of Flowers, another bell jingles over the door. **DING-A-LING!**

This store smells nice too, but Mr. Roeser's roses don't compare to donuts!

There is a pretty blond sales lady at the counter sprinkling glitter over a bouquet of lilies. A short guy with glasses ties a red ribbon around the stems and places the flowers into a vase.

"Welcome to the Little Shop of Flowers," says the lady. "I'm Audrey, and this is Seymour."

"Nice to meet you," I say to them. "I'm Billy Burger, and this is my dad. Is Mr. Roeser around? I'd like to ask him a question."

"Sure!" Audrey replies. "He's down in the office."

She picks up the nearby telephone and calls her boss.

Seymour politely excuses himself to get some more supplies.

Dad and I look around the store and see one of the windows has recently been replaced, but the sill and pane are cracked and damaged.

"Every garden has a few weeds, I'm afraid," says a voice behind us.

Dad and I turn to see Mr. Roeser, a tall, thin man with a bright smile.

"How may I help you?" he asks.

I tell him about the Jump-a-thon and my search for sponsors.

Suddenly Seymour comes clomping up the stairs carrying a bag of peat moss. He trips over his untied shoelace and plops face first.

SPLAT!

Audrey rushes over with a broom and dustpan to help him.

"Sorry, Mr. Roeser," Seymour says. "I'm a little bit accident prone."

"No use crying over spilled dirt, my boy," Mr. Roeser replies. "Just put it in the bag!"

While Seymour and Audrey clean up the mess, the bell over the shop door rings again. **DING-A-LING!** I turn around to see who it is. It's Teddy with his dad.

Teddy is also holding his sponsor sheet and pamphlets. His dad is holding a paper coffee cup with the House of Sweets logo on it.

My friend and I look at each other and have a sudden realization. We are both after the same sponsors!

Oh, no! Time to strike fast and quick.

"Hello, *Theodore*," I say, using Teddy's full name. He hates when I do that.

"Hello, *William*," he says, using my full name. I hate when he does that.

"This here is my territory," I tell him. It sounds like something out of one of Dad's old cowboy movies.

"Oh, really?" Teddy snaps back. "I don't see your name written anywhere."

"Actually, my name is chiseled onto that fountain out there," I say.

"That's your grandfathers' name," Teddy says.

"Well, we have the same name!" I shout.

"All right, boys," Mr. Roeser says, coming between us. "I'm just going to nip this in the bud right now."

"You're right, Mr. Roeser," I tell the florist. "I shouldn't be fighting when I'm trying to better myself."

"Better yourself?" Mr. Roeser asks.

"Yeah," I say. "I'm trying to be a model citizen like my grandfather and inspire people to do good. I'm doing this fund-raiser to help people take care of their health the same way I'm trying to take care of mine."

Mr. Roeser smiles wide and says, "Why, that is a very impressive statement, young man. I would be honored to sponsor you!"

"Thank you," I say and hand him a pamphlet.

He opens the register and pulls out some money.

"Count me in," Seymour says. "And Audrey too!"

As the nice flower shop workers reach for their cash, I lean over and whisper in Teddy's ear. "You're not the only actor around here, buddy," I say.

Teddy sticks his tongue out at me and then quickly puts on his bright, cheery face. He holds up his sponsor sheet and yells, "I'm trying to better myself too!"

● ● ●

After the flower shop, my dad and I run to the photography studio next door and then to the art supply store. We are one step ahead of Teddy and his father, but we're running out of stores in the shopping center.

"DAAAD!" I complain. "Teddy's gonna have the same amount of sponsors as me! We gotta do something. Let's go to the costume shop and buy disguises. Then we can start all over again and no one will know!"

"Billy!" Dad says sternly.

But then he puts his hand on my shoulder and starts rubbing his chin. He does that when he's thinking.

"I have a plan!" he says. "We are going back to the House of Sweets after all!"

"But what about our disguises?" I ask.

"We won't need disguises to get some donuts."

"*Hmm*, I like where this is going," I tell my father, "but donuts aren't going to help me get ahead of Teddy."

"It is if we share it with my buddies at the precinct," Dad replies with a wink. "It's just the thing to sweeten them up when you ask for more sponsors!"

My eyes go wide. There's like a hundred police officers in there.

"Dad, you're a genius!" I tell him. "Now I see where I get it from."

⑩
Jump Day

After what seems like forever, the day of the Jump-a-thon finally arrives. I don't think I've ever wanted to go to school this badly in my entire life.

I get dressed, eat breakfast, and run to the bus stop in a flash. My new name should be Billy *Blur*-ger!

Teddy shows up a minute later. We are both wearing our gym clothes, which was one of the requirements for the Jump-a-thon.

"Are you as excited as I am?" I ask.

"Oh, yeah," he replies. "I'll be even more excited after I win that trip to Adventuretown!"

Before I can come back with a snappy response, the bus arrives. Instead I just say, "May the best man win."

When we get on the bus, everyone is talking about the Jump-a-thon.

I think about how Mom, Dad, and I had been exercising together to Robert Summers videos for the last couple of days.

"Hey, you wanna know something?" I say to Teddy. "I'm no longer eating junk food, and my pants finally fit me again without the buttons popping off."

"That's awesome, dude," he says. "Now I don't have to wear a helmet next time I come over."

• • •

As soon as we arrive at school, Principal Crank and the teachers are waiting to escort us into the gymnasium. There is a big stage in the front where a crew is setting up live instruments. My friends and I walk over to get a closer look.

"Whoa, cool!" I exclaim.

A long banner that reads "ANNUAL JUMP-A-THON" hangs overhead. On both sides of the banner, there are posters of Robert Summers and his band, the Jumping Jacks.

"This is going to be awesome!" Teddy says.

"This is going to be epic!" says Jason.

"This is going to be awesomely epic!" says Michael. We all agree.

Once all the students and faculty are gathered, Principal Crank stands on the stage.

"Good morning, all, and thank you for your participation in today's festive event. Please have your sponsor sheets and money envelopes ready. Volunteers from KHIX FM are going around to collect them. The money will be placed in this large trunk at the edge of the stage for our judges to tally up the contributions."

As the principal is speaking, people dressed in white KHIX T-shirts come around and take our envelopes before handing us an official KHIX jump rope.

Soon, Principal Crank is joined onstage by a woman with pink hair, several earrings, and tattoos on her arms. Some of the older students start squealing and clapping.

"And now, without further ado," Principal Crank states. "It is my pleasure to welcome radio host of Rock Your Socks Off and former Fork Lane School student, our very own Ms. Stephanie Gwen!"

There is a round of applause and Stephanie takes the microphone.

"Thanks, Crank!" she says. "I gotta say, it's great to be back at Fork Lane School. This is a great place. Music class was my favorite. It helped me find my passion and do what I love at KHIX FM. It was a pleasant surprise when Principal Crank asked me to host the Jump-a-thon. It was the one time he came to my office, instead of me going to his. **HA-HA!**"

Everyone laughs at Stephanie's joke. Here's another troublemaker doing something good, just like me!

When the audience quiets down, Stephanie asks, "Are you ready to rock your socks off?"

"YES!" we scream.

"Then give it up for rockin' Robert Summers and the Jumping Jacks!"

The crowd goes wild as a muscular man in shorts, a T-shirt, and a headband cartwheels onto the stage. Behind him, another muscular man and two fit women in similar outfits also cartwheel onto the stage. They take up the electric guitar, the bass, and the drums while Stephanie hands the microphone to Robert.

"LET'S GET JUMPIN'!" he shouts.

The band breaks into a fast-paced dance number. Robert sings while everyone jump ropes.

Some kids are jumping fast with the music, while others are showing off their jump-rope skills by doing neat tricks like hopping on one foot or crisscrossing the rope.

I don't know any jump-rope tricks, so I just stick to keeping my rhythm slow and steady.

After a few minutes, some kids stop and go sit on the benches to catch their breaths. Teddy and I are still going strong.

I can feel my leg muscles burning and my heart pumping, but I'm not stopping. This is too much fun.

Finally, at the end of the performance, Stephanie comes back onstage with her own microphone.

"You guys are looking great out there, but it's time for the moment you've all been waiting for. It's time to announce our winner!"

This is it, I think. *First prize*. I can almost feel the wind whipping through my hair on the biggest roller coaster at Adventuretown.

Stephanie hands a sheet of paper to Robert and asks, "Will you do the honor?"

"Gladly!" he replies. "It says here that the winner is a third grader from Mr. Karas's class!"

My classmates and I cheer.

"SAY WHAT?!" I exclaim.

This may actually happen.

First prize is nearly mine!

I cross my fingers as Robert unfolds the paper.

"And the winner is . . ."

11
Billy Burger: Model Citizen

"Polly Pemberton!" announces Robert Summers.

Teddy and I hang our heads as Polly's high-pitched shriek pierces through the gym.

"OHMYGOSH, OHMYGOSH, OHMYGOSH," she sputters, running onto the stage to collect her prize.

"Aw, man!" I shout.

I kick the gym floor and leave a scuff mark from my sneaker. Oops. I quickly rub it away with my shoe before anyone notices it.

While everyone else crowds around the stage to **OOH** and **AAH** over Polly and her prize, Teddy and I walk over to the water station.

The volunteers hand us each a paper cup full of water.

"Losing sure makes me thirsty," Teddy says.

"Hey, we tried and we had fun, and I wish Polly the best," I reply.

PFFT! Teddy spits out his water.

"Who are you and what have you done with my best friend?" he ask.

"Ha-ha, just kidding," I say. "I hope she barfs on a roller coaster."

Teddy laughs. "That's better."

As my friend and I throw our empty cups into the recycle bin, we hear another high-pitched scream.

"AIEEEEEEEEEEEE!"

Only this time it's not Polly.

It's Stephanie Gwen!

"Somebody stop them!" she shouts into her microphone.

Teddy and I whirl around to see a startling scene.

Three hooded figures jump off the stage and push their way through the crowd. One of them is waving a baseball bat. The other two are carrying the trunk full of money!

We watch as the one swinging the bat knocks over a table full of pamphlets and T-shirts.

WHACK!

"Billy, look!" Teddy shouts. "They're stealing all of our funds!"

"No more stealing," I exclaim. "Not in my school!"

The three thieves make a break for the nearest exit. Only two things stand in their way. Teddy and I.

"I have an idea," I tell Teddy. "Here, hold this."

I hand him one handle of my jump rope and run away from him while holding the other. I stop when the rope springs tight between us.

At that very moment, the bat-wielding thug comes hurtling toward us.

"Sweep the leg!" I shout.

Teddy and I swing the rope down, causing the crook to trip over it. He stumbles and tumbles headfirst onto the gym floor.

SLAM!

The baseball bat slips from his grip. It slides under the feet of his friends, and the other two trip and fall. They land on top of the first thief, and the trunk lands on top of them.

THUD!

With the dazed criminals sprawled on their stomachs, Teddy and I can clearly see the fiery emblem stitched on the back. It's the Hicksville Comets symbol . . . just like the ones from the video at the bakery.

"Whoa," I say. "I think this is them."

"Who?" Teddy asks.

"The crooks who robbed all those stores in the town square," I reply. "I think we solved the case!"

Before the three thieves can get back on their feet, Principal Crank arrives with Robert Summers and Stephanie Gwen.

Each of them picks up a thief off the floor.

"They're just teenagers," Robert says, looking at their faces.

"They're troublemakers!" shouts Principal Crank. "And I'm taking them to my office until the police come to claim them!"

"I still remember the way," Stephanie says. "Follow me." The three adults exit the gymnasium with the teens in tow.

My heart is beating faster than before, and my legs are trembling and shaking like jelly. I sit on the trunk to catch my breath.

Suddenly a rush of people crowd around Teddy and me. It's so loud and noisy that my head is spinning.

Jason and Michael make it to the front and yell, "Dudes, that was epically awesome! You guys are totally heroes!"

"Ha!" I laugh. "I guess I do know some jump-rope tricks after all."

Teddy and I high-five.

Finally, Mr. Karas clears a path and gets everyone to calm down. He is joined by Robert Summers and Stephanie Gwen.

When there is silence, he asks us if we are all right.

"Oh, sure," I say, shrugging. "All in a day's work."

"Billy, what you and your friend did was very brave and heroic," Stephanie says. "You, young man, are a model citizen!"

I blush.

"And thanks to you, all the money that was raised will still help fund research for heart health," Robert adds. "And so, to show you our appreciation, Stephanie and I would love to join both you and your families for an all-expenses-paid day of fitness and fun at . . . **ADVENTURETOWN**!"

Teddy and I jump up and shout, **"SAY WHAT?!"**

Wow, I think. *What an awesome day!*

I can't wait to go home and tell my family.

Dad is gonna be so psyched that I helped catch the crooks.

Grandma is gonna be so proud that I helped my community.

Oh, and Mom is gonna flip out when she meets Robert Summers.

About the Author

New York Times best-selling author John Sazaklis enjoys writing children's books about his favorite characters. He has also illustrated Spider-Man books and created toys used in *MAD Magazine*. To him, it's a dream come true! John lives with his family in New York City.

About the Illustrator

Lee Robinson grew up in a small town in England. As a child, he wasn't a strong reader, but the art in books always caught his eye. He loved to see how the characters came to life. He decided to become an illustrator so he could create worlds of characters himself. In addition to illustrating books and comic books, Lee runs workshops to help teach kids about literacy, art, and creativity through comics.

WHAT DO YOU THINK?

QUESTIONS TO THINK, TALK, AND WRITE ABOUT

1. What is a model citizen? Do you know any model citizens? Write about him or her.

2. Do you think that Billy was aware of what he was doing when he stole the chips? Use the details from the book to support your answer.

3. The Burger family worked on having healthier habits. Choose a health habit—either one from the book or one of your own—and write a paragraph about it.

4. Reread the scene where Billy's button pops off his pants (pages 19-21) Then create a comic retelling this scene. Use speech bubbles for dialogue, and don't forget sound effects!

5. Pretend you are a reporter and you have been assigned a story about the near robbery at the Jump-a-thon. Write your story, and don't forget to include Billy and Teddy's thoughts on the event.

Billy's Glossary

antics—wild and funny actions . . . at least I think they are funny

caper—a sort of naughty, maybe even illegal, action; Think stealing potato chips

chiseled—cut or carved into something

dedicated—put someone's name on something in their honor

disguises—things you wear that hide who you really are

epic—super awesome; Probably more awesome than anything you've ever seen

galaxy—a super huge group of stars and planets; Our galaxy is the Milky Way, which honestly makes me a little hungry

hooligans—rotten people; I know that Principal Crank might think I'm a hooligan, but I swear I'm not that bad

inhale—to breathe in; When you inhale food, it is like you don't even waste time chewing

mesmerizing—so amazing that you can't think straight; The chip bags mesmerized me right into stealing

miserable—sad times a billion

mission—a special job that needs to get done

mutants—people or animals that change from their normal form into monsters

obvious—so clear that anyone can see it

reputation—your reputation is how you come across to others; Clearly, my reputation is "cool guy"

saliva—a fancier word for spit

sodium—this has to do with how much salt is in something; Low-sodium turkey is not as bad as I expected it to be, but please don't tell anyone I admitted that

starved—suffered greatly from a lack of food; I starve at least once a day

surrender—give up, end of story

suspiciously—if you do something suspiciously, you have a feeling that something shady is happening

territory—a certain area; Note: stay out of enemy territory

universe—everything in space; We're talking the planets, stars, moons . . . you get the picture

JOSHUA WILLIAMS

A REAL-LIFE MODEL CITIZEN

When Joshua Williams was four-and-a-half years old, he noticed a homeless man asking for help. Joshua wanted to give him some of his own spending money. His grandma had just given him $20, so he happily gave it to the man in need.

Joshua continued to think about people who don't have enough food to eat. "They're not as fortunate as we are," Joshua said. "So I wanted to help them."

Some of Joshua's family decided to help Joshua with his mission. At first they served the hungry by serving hot meals to homeless people in their area. Later they started giving bags of groceries to those in need.

After two years, they formed Joshua's Heart Foundation. Now Joshua and his organization work to end hunger worldwide. So far, they have provided more than one million pounds of food to those in need in Florida, Jamaica, Africa, and India.

Joshua isn't the only young person involved in his charity. More than 5,000 volunteers, called elves, help fight hunger with fund-raisers and other efforts throughout the country. "I am calling on all young people to help me to fight hunger," Joshua writes. **"HELP ME TO CREATE AWARENESS. TOGETHER WE CAN ACHIEVE THE IMPOSSIBLE."**

To get involved, visit www.joshuasheart.org.